A GOLDEN BOOK • NEW YORK

Compilation copyright © 2017 by Penguin Random House LLC.
All rights reserved. This 2017 edition was published in the United States by Golden Books, an imprint of Random House Children's Books,
a division of Penguin Random House LLC, 1745 Broadway, New York, NY 10019. Golden Books, A Golden Book,
A Little Golden Book, the G colophon, and the distinctive gold spine are registered trademarks
of Penguin Random House LLC. A Little Golden Book Classic is a trademark of Penguin Random House LLC.
Scuffy the Tugboat and The Saggy Baggy Elephant are trademarks of Penguin Random House LLC.
The works that appear herein were originally published separately as the following:
Scuffy the Tugboat and His Adventures Down the River copyright © 1946, 1955, renewed 1974, 1983 by Penguin Random House LLC.
The Saggy Baggy Elephant copyright © 1947, renewed 1975 by Penguin Random House LLC.
The Sailor Dog copyright © 1953, renewed 1981 by Penguin Random House LLC.
randomhousekids.com
Educators and librarians, for a variety of teaching tools, visit us at
RHTeachersLibrarians.com
ISBN 978-0-375-97610-0

This special edition was printed for Kohl's Department Stores, Inc.
(for distribution on behalf of Kohl's Cares, LLC, its wholly owned subsidiary)
by Random House Children's Books, a division of Penguin Random House LLC, New York.

KOHL'S
Style 97610
Factory Number 126509
Production Date 01/2017

Ages 3 and up

MANUFACTURED IN CHINA
10 9 8 7 6 5 4 3 2 1

THE SAGGY BAGGY ELEPHANT

by K. & B. JACKSON

illustrated by GUSTAF TENGGREN

A happy little elephant was dancing through the jungle. He thought he was dancing beautifully, one-two-three-kick. But whenever he went one-two-three, his big feet pounded so that they shook the whole jungle. And whenever he went kick, he kicked over a tree or a bush.

The little elephant danced along leaving wreckage behind him, until one day, he met a parrot.

"Why are you shaking the jungle all to pieces?" cried the parrot, who had never before seen an elephant. "What kind of animal are you, anyway?"

The little elephant said, "I don't know what kind of animal I am. I live all alone in the jungle. I dance and I kick—and I call myself Sooki. It's a good-sounding name, and it fits me, don't you think?"

"Maybe," answered the parrot, "but if it does it's the only thing that *does* fit you. Your ears are too big for you, and your nose is way too big for you. And your skin is *much,* MUCH too big for you. It's baggy and saggy. You should call yourself Saggy-Baggy!"

Sooki sighed. His pants *did* look pretty wrinkled.

"I'd be glad to improve myself," he said, "but I don't know how to go about it. What shall I do?"

"I can't tell you. I never saw anything like you in all my life!" replied the parrot.

The little elephant tried to smooth out his skin.
He rubbed it with his trunk. That did no good.

He pulled up his pants legs—but they fell right back into dozens of wrinkles.

It was very disappointing, and the parrot's saucy laugh didn't help a bit.

Just then a tiger came walking along. He was a beautiful, sleek tiger. His skin fit him like a glove.

Sooki rushed up
to him and said:
"Tiger, please
tell me why your
skin fits so well!
The parrot says
mine is all baggy
and saggy, and I do
want to make it fit me like yours fits you!"

The tiger didn't care a fig about Sooki's
troubles, but he did feel flattered and
important, and he did feel just a little mite
hungry.

"My skin always did fit," said the tiger.
"Maybe it's because I take a lot of exercise.
But . . ." added the tiger, ". . . if you don't
care for exercise, I shall be delighted to nibble
a few of those extra pounds of skin off for
you!"

"Oh no, thank you! No, thank you!" cried
Sooki. "I love exercise! Just watch me!"

Sooki ran until he was well beyond reach.

Then he did somersaults and rolled on his back. He walked on his hind legs and he walked on his front legs.

When Sooki wandered down to the river to get a big drink of water, he met the parrot. The parrot laughed harder than ever.

"I tried exercising," sighed the little elephant. "Now I don't know what to do."

"Soak in the water the way the crocodile does," laughed the parrot. "Maybe your skin will shrink."

So Sooki tramped straight into the water.

But before he had soaked nearly long enough to shrink his skin, a great big crocodile came swimming up, snapping his fierce jaws and looking greedily at Sooki's tender ears.

The little elephant clambered up the bank and ran away, feeling very discouraged.

"I'd better hide in a dark place where my bags and sags and creases and wrinkles won't show," he said.

By and by he found a deep dark cave, and with a heavy sigh he tramped inside and sat down.

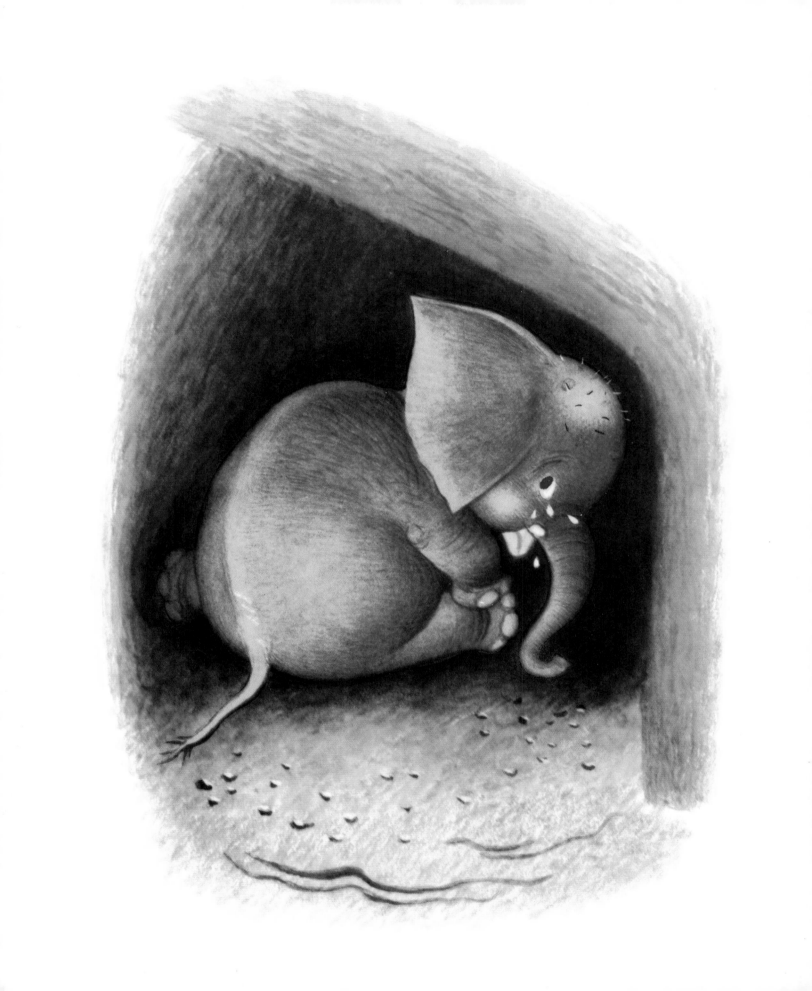

Suddenly, he heard a fierce growling and grumbling and snarling. He peeped out of the cave and saw a lion padding down the path.

"I'm hungry!" roared the lion. "I haven't had a thing to eat today. Not a thing except a thin, bony antelope, and a puny monkey—and a buffalo, but such a tough one! And two turtles, but you can't count turtles. There's nothing much to eat between those saucers they wear for clothes! I'm *hungry!* I could eat an *elephant!*"

And he began to pad straight toward the dark cave where the little elephant was hidden.

"This is the end of me, sags, bags, wrinkles and all," thought Sooki, and he let out one last, trumpeting bellow!

Just as he did, the jungle was filled with a
terrible crashing and an awful stomping. A whole
herd of great gray wrinkled elephants came
charging up, and the big hungry lion jumped up
in the air, turned around, and ran away as fast as
he could go.

Sooki peeped out of the cave and all the big
elephants smiled at him. Sooki thought they were
the most beautiful creatures he had ever seen.

"I wish I looked just like you," he said.

"You do," grinned the big elephants. "You're a perfectly dandy little elephant!"

And that made Sooki so happy that he began to

dance one-two-three-kick through the jungle, with
all those big, brave, friendly elephants behind him.
The saucy parrot watched them dance. But this
time he didn't laugh, not even to himself.

THE SAILOR DOG

by MARGARET WISE BROWN

illustrated by GARTH WILLIAMS

Born at sea in the teeth of a gale, the
sailor was a dog. Scuppers was his name.

After that he lived on a farm. But Scuppers,
born at sea, was a sailor. And when he grew
up, he wanted to go to sea.

So he went to look for something to go in.
He found a little submarine. "All aboard!"
they called. It was going down under the sea.
But Scuppers did not want to go under the sea.

He found a little car.
"All aboard!" they called. It was going over the land. But Scuppers did not want to go over the land.

Scuppers was a sailor. He wanted to go to sea.

So Scuppers went over the hills and far away
until he came to the sea.

Over the hills and far away was the ocean.
And on the ocean was a ship. The ship was about
to go over the sea. It blew all its whistles.

"All aboard!" they called.

"All ashore that are going ashore!"

"All aboard!"

So Scuppers went to sea.

The ship began to move slowly along. The wind blew it.

In his ship Scuppers had a little room. In his room Scuppers had a hook for his hat and a hook for his rope and a hook for his handkerchief and a hook for his pants and a hook for his spyglass and a place for his shoes and a bunk for a bed to put himself in.

At night Scuppers threw the anchor into
the sea, and he went down to his little room.

He put his hat on the hook for his hat, and his rope on the hook for his rope, and his pants on the hook for his pants, and his spyglass on the hook for his spyglass, and he put his shoes under the bed and got into his bed, which was a bunk, and went to sleep.

Next morning he was shipwrecked.
Too big a storm blew out of the sky. The
anchor dragged, and the ship crashed onto
the rocks. There was a big hole in it.
Scuppers himself was washed overboard
and hurled by huge waves onto the shore.

He was washed up onto the beach.
It was foggy and rainy. There were no
houses, and Scuppers needed a house.
But on the beach was lots and lots of
driftwood, and he found an old rusty box
stuck in the sand.
Maybe it was a treasure!

It was a treasure—to Scuppers.

It was an old-fashioned tool box with hammers and nails and an ax and a saw. Everything he needed to build himself a house. So Scuppers started to build a house, all by himself, out of driftwood.

He built a door and a window and a roof and a porch and a floor, all out of driftwood.

And he found some red bricks and built a big red chimney. And then he lit a fire, and the smoke went up the chimney.

Then the stars came out, and he was sleepy.
So he built a bed of pine branches.
    And he jumped into his deep green bed
and went to sleep. As he slept he dreamed—

If he could build a house,
he could mend the hole in the ship.

So the next day at low tide he took his tool box and waded out and hammered planks across the hole in his ship.

At last the ship was fixed.

So he sailed away.

Until he came to a seaport in a foreign land.

By now his clothes were all worn and ripped and torn and blown to pieces. His coat was torn, his hat was blown away, and his shoes were all worn out. And his handkerchief was ripped. Only his pants were still good.

So he went ashore to buy some clothes at the Army and Navy Store. And some fresh oranges. He bought a coat. He found a red one too small. He found a blue one just right. It had brass buttons on it.

Then he went to buy a hat. He found a purple one too silly. He found a white one just right.

He needed new shoes. He found some yellow ones too small. He found some red ones too fancy. Then he found some white ones just right.

Here he is with his new hat on, and with his new shoes on, and with his new coat on, with his shiny brass buttons. (He has a can of polish and a cloth to keep them shiny.)

And he has a new clean handkerchief, and a new rope, and a bushel of oranges.

And now Scuppers wants to go back to his ship. So he goes there.

And at night when the stars came out, he took one last look through his spyglass. And went down below to his little room, and he hung his new hat on the hook for his hat, and he hung his spyglass on the hook for his spyglass, and he hung his new coat on the hook for his coat, and his new handkerchief on the hook for his handkerchief, and his pants on the hook for his pants, and his new rope on the hook for his rope, and his new shoes he put under his bunk, and himself he put in his bunk.

And here he is where he wants to be— a sailor sailing the deep green sea.

HIS SONG

I am Scuppers the Sailor Dog—
I'm Scuppers the Sailor Dog—
I can sail in a gale
right over a whale
under full sail
in a fog.

I am Scuppers the Sailor Dog—
I'm Scuppers the Sailor Dog—
with a shake and a snort
I can sail into port
under full sail
in a fog.

Scuffy
THE TUGBOAT

by GERTRUDE CRAMPTON

illustrated by TIBOR GERGELY

Scuffy was sad.
Scuffy was cross.
Scuffy sniffed his blue smokestack.

"A toy store is no place for a red-painted tugboat," said Scuffy, and he sniffed his blue smokestack again. "I was meant for bigger things."

"Perhaps you would not be cross if you went sailing," said the man with the polka dot tie, who owned the shop.

So one night he took Scuffy home to his little boy. He filled the bathtub with water.

"Sail, little tugboat," said the little boy.

"I won't sail in a bathtub," said Scuffy. "A tub is no place for a red-painted tugboat. I was meant for bigger things."

The next day the man with the polka dot tie and his little boy carried Scuffy to a laughing brook that started high in the hills.

"Sail, little tugboat," said the man with the polka dot tie.

It was Spring, and the brook was full
to the brim with its water. And the water
moved in a hurry, as all things move in a
hurry when it is Spring.
 Scuffy was in a hurry, too.

"Come back, little tugboat, come back," cried the little boy as the hurrying, brimful brook carried Scuffy downstream.

"Not I," tooted Scuffy. "Not I. This is the life for me."

All that day Scuffy sailed along with the brook.
Past the meadows filled with cowslips. Past the
women washing clothes on the bank. Past the
little woods filled with violets.

Cows came to the brook to drink.

They stood in the cool water, and it was fun

to sail around between their legs and bump softly
into their noses.

It was fun to see them drink.

But when a white and brown cow almost drank
Scuffy instead of the brook's cool water, Scuffy
was frightened. That was not fun!

Night came, and with it the moon.
There was nothing to see but the quiet trees.
Suddenly an owl called out, "Hoot! Hooot!"
"Toot, tooot!" cried the frightened tugboat,
and he wished he could see the smiling face of
the man with the polka dot tie.

When morning came, Scuffy was cross instead of frightened.

"I was meant for bigger things, but which way am I to go?" he said. But there was only one way to go, and that was with the running water where the two brooks met to form a small river. And with the river sailed Scuffy, the red-painted tugboat.

He was proud when he sailed past villages.
"People build villages at the edge of my
river," said Scuffy, and he straightened his
blue smokestack.

Once Scuffy's river joined a small one jammed with logs. Here were men in heavy jackets and great boots, walking about on the floating logs, trying to pry them free.

"Toot, toot, let me through," demanded Scuffy. But the men paid no attention to him. They pushed the logs apart so they would drift with the river to the sawmill in the town. Scuffy bumped along with the jostling logs.

"Ouch!" he cried as two logs bumped together.

"This is a fine river," said Scuffy, "but it's very busy and very big for me."

He was proud when he sailed under the bridges.

"My river is so wide and so deep that people must build bridges to cross it."

The river moved through big towns now instead of villages.

And the bridges over it were very wide—
wide enough so that many cars and trucks
and streetcars could cross all at once.

The river got deeper and deeper. Scuffy
did not have to tuck up his bottom.

The river moved faster and faster.

"I feel like a train instead of a tugboat,"
said Scuffy, as he was hurried along.

He was proud when he passed the old
sawmill with its water wheel.

But high in the hills and mountains the winter snow melted. Water filled the brooks and rushed from there into the small rivers. Faster and faster it flowed, to the great river where Scuffy sailed.

"There is too much water in this river," said Scuffy, as he pitched and tossed on the waves. "Soon it will splash over the top and what a flood there will be!"

Soon great armies of men came to save the fields and towns from the rushing water.

They filled bags with sand and put them at the edge of the river.

"They're making higher banks for the river," shouted Scuffy, "to hold the water back." The water rose higher and higher.

The men built the sand bags higher and higher. Higher! went the river. Higher! went the sand bags.

At last the water rose no more. The flood water rushed on to the sea, and Scuffy raced along with the flood. The people and the fields and the towns were safe.

On went the river to the sea. At last Scuffy
sailed into a big city. Here the river widened,
and all about were docks and wharves.

Oh, it was a busy place and a noisy place!
The cranes groaned as they swung the cargoes
into great ships. The porters shouted as they
carried suitcases and boxes on board.

Horses stamped and truck motors roared,
streetcars clanged and people shouted. Scuffy
said, "Toot, toot," but nobody noticed.

"Oh, oh!" cried Scuffy when he saw the sea. "There is no beginning and there is no end to the sea. I wish I could find the man with the polka dot tie and his little boy!"

Just as the little red-painted tugboat sailed past the last piece of land, a hand reached out and picked him up. And there was the man with the polka dot tie, with his little boy beside him.

Scuffy is home now with the man with the polka dot tie and his little boy.

He sails from one end of the bathtub to the other.

"This is the place for a red-painted tugboat," said Scuffy. "And this is the life for me."